The Night JESUS CHRIST Returned to Earth

-Captain Tom Hudgens

Copyrighted: October 1999

Publisher
BILR Corporation
P.O. Box 102276
Denver CO 80250-2276

ISBN 0-937177-01-6
Library of Congress Catalog Card Number: 99-091461

INDEX

FOREWORD

What will Jesus say when He returns to Earth in person? He has been expected many, many times. Suppose He does arrive at the arrival of the Third Millennium. What will He say? Here is what I think He will say.

In this book I have intentionally put words into Jesus' mouth. Whether the words came directly to me from Him or that the words are my own invention is debatable. But I believe in all that I have printed as His words. I believe His whole ministry was based on love, peace, and ethical behavior, plus forgiveness.

I am not predicting that Jesus will arrive on New Year's Eve, but if we believe in miracles this could happen in the manner I describe.

If what I have Jesus say in this book does not agree with what you think He would say, I challenge you to write down what you think He would endorse today.

All the quotes from the Bible are taken from The New Revised Standard Version of the Holy Bible.

THE NIGHT JESUS CHRIST RETURNED TO EARTH

2

COMMANDMENTS ONE & TWO - PRESIDENT JIM BUCKS

"I am the Lord your God; .... You shall have no other gods before me." Exodus 20:2,3

"You shall not make for yourself an idol, whether in the form of anything that is in heaven above, or that is on the earth beneath, or that is in the water under the earth ......"
Exodus 20:4

"Constance, phone our Board Chairman for me, and as soon as I have finished that call, phone my wife for me."

Jim Bucks in his office in Manhattan overlooking the East River has just completed with deep interest a study of the latest financial statement of his company. He had worked hard to bring this company out of the red and into a Fortune 500 Company with outstanding profits. His shareholders and Board of Directors will be delighted with this latest statement. They were kind enough to have voted him stock options when he joined the company, plus five million dollars annual salary. The options are now worth twenty million dollars. Of course he did feel badly about his having to let ten thousand workers go in the downsizing of the company. This produced less customer satisfaction, Union threats, and worker discontent and fear for the remaining jobs. The bottom line, however, stands out as a remarkable success story in the eyes of his peers.

He would now retire and would ask his shareholders and Board Members to prepare a "Golden Parachute" for him for his retirement. This would reward him for all he had done to make this company so profitable. A forty million-dollar "Golden Parachute" would not be too much to ask for, he thought, since he had made billions for this company. He knew his Board Members would support this because they each would like a similar deal for themselves. No matter the widening gulf between the rich and the poor in this country. Everyone had to look after himself or herself nowadays.

At age 51, after retirement from this company, he could still take on another company to repeat this process of milking money from the workers, shareholders, and the company.

The call to the Chairman was brief and to the point, for the Chairman was a longtime friend. He readily agreed to Bucks' plan.

When Jim had Denise, his wife, on the phone he said, "Tomorrow night is the dawn of the new millennium. We are invited to sit on the speakers' platform in Times Square, for the big celebration. Dress in your best clothes."

COMMANDMENT THREE -
COACH DALE McGRUFF

"You shall not make wrongful use of the name of the Lord
your God ...." Exodus 20:7

"Men, we are up against a goddamn good team this coming New Year's Day. You will have to kick their butts and play a hell of a lot harder than you have in any other game we have played."

Dale McGruff was addressing his football team players at the last day of practice before the national championship game. He had become the best-known college coach in the country, for on Christmas Day, 1999, his team had overwhelmed their opponent in the national championship race. The team would be facing its final opponent on New Year's Day, 2000 just after the big celebration of the dawn of the new millennium at Times Square.

Dale was noted for his temper and his foul language. In spite of this he was a technocrat at football. He had reintroduced a double wing back formation that Knute Rochne had used at Notre Dame in the 1930's. It became very successful with its ability to hide the football from the defensive opponents. Was it this new formation or Dale's temper and language that brought forth such a great football team?

Dale continued in his talk to his team, "I want you to be the first goddamn team and me the first goddamn coach to win the championship in the new millennium. I plan to be in Times Square at midnight tomorrow night for the big celebration, but I want all of you to be in bed getting a hell of a good night's rest for the game. Then get in there Saturday and fight your goddamn heart out for the glory of your school and for all of us."

COMMANDMENT FOUR -
LARRY MILWORTH

"Remember the Sabbath day, and keep it holy. Six days you shall labor, and do all your work. But the seventh day is a Sabbath to the Lord your God; you shall not do any work....." Exodus 20:8,9,10

"Dad, can we play some catch today with our new baseball gloves Aunt Matilda gave us for Christmas?" eight year old David asked his father.

"Not today, David," replied his father, Larry Milworth, "I am making a cabinet for a customer down the block. He didn't even ask how much it would cost. We can use the money to buy extra baseball equipment."

Larry did not notice the look of dejection on David's face as he turned around and left the workshop.

Larry Milworth is a workaholic. He never takes time to "smell the roses". Five days a week he is a mechanic, and weekends he is a landscaper. He never has time with his wife and children, because at home he is always working on some project with his woodworking tools. In essence he has three jobs. He is not suffering from lack of money. He provides well for his family as far as covering all necessities of life, with plenty left over. At times, he appears tired and haggard. But the one night that he always keeps open is New Year's Eve. He and his wife Alice are planning to help bring in the dawn of a new millennium in Times Square.

COMMANDMENT FIVE -
TEENAGER WALT BRASH

"Honor your father and your mother, so that your days may be long on the land that the Lord your God is giving you." Exodus 20:12

Teenager Walt Brash responded to his acquaintance Rod from another school after being questioned by Rod as to where he had been the past few weeks.

"My old man grounded me for a month for taking his car without his permission. He wasn't using it, so I didn't see why he would care about my taking it. I needed it to attend the Kegger in Rogers Park last month. I had just received my driver's license six weeks ago and I was taking three other boys who don't yet have their licenses.

"Well, I was only driving 65 in a 45 mph zone when a dog darted across the road in front of me. I tried to miss him by jerking the car right. I lost control and ran off the road into a tree. I guess the beer was too much for me. My friend in the front seat did not have on his seat belt. He was thrown into the windshield, and is still in the hospital recovering from his injuries. The other two and I fortunately had on our seat belts and suffered only minor injuries. Anyway, my month is up today. My family and I are going to the celebration at Times Square tonight."

COMMANDMENT SIX - GENERAL WESTMASTER

"You shall not murder." Exodus 20:13

"We have won the war. That is the main lesson to come from our recent conflict."

This was the gist of General Westmaster's address to various organizations. He was at the height of his military career. He had successfully led his country and its allies in a recent conflict in Europe. It deeply concerned him that so many thousands of people were killed, raped, and /or displaced to become refugees. He knew the world must find a better way to settle international disputes to prevent such carnage as this.

In his mind General Westmaster had already conceived of a better way, but he would have to move carefully to implement it. He would spend the rest of his life to help bring about the abolition of war. Statements of three deceased American generals, General & President Ulysses S. Grant, General Douglas MacArthur, and General & President Dwight D. Eisenhower, had inspired him.

GENERAL ULYSSES S. GRANT

"I am convinced that the Great Framer of the world will so develop it that it becomes one nation, so that armies and navies are no longer necessary."

"I believe at some future day, the nations of the earth will agree upon some sort of congress which will take cognizance of international questions of difficulty and whose decisions will be as binding as the decisions of our Supreme Court are upon us."

GENERAL DOUGLAS MacARTHUR

"Abolition of war is no longer an ethical question to be pondered solely by learned philosophers and ecclesiastics, but a hard core one for the decision of the masses whose survival is the issue. Many will tell you with mockery and ridicule that the abolition of war can only be a dream.....that it is the vague imagining of a visionary. But we must go on or we will go under! We must have new thoughts, new ideas, new concepts. We must break out of the straitjacket of the past. We must have sufficient imaginations and courage to translate the universal wish for peace - which is rapidly becoming a universal necessity - into actuality."

"The very triumph of scientific annihilation has destroyed the possibility of war being a medium of practical settlement of international differences.....If you lose, you are annihilated. If you win, you stand only to lose. War contains the germs of double suicide....Military alliances, balances of power, leagues of nations – all in turn have failed......We have our last chance. If we will not devise some greater and more equitable system, Armageddon will be at our door."

GENERAL DWIGHT D. EISENHOWER

".....What is the true security problem of the day? That problem is not merely man against man or nation against nation. It is man against war."

"When we get to the point, as we one day will, that both sides know that in any outbreak of general hostilities, regardless of the element of surprise, destruction will be both reciprocal and complete, possibly we will have sense enough to meet at the conference table with the understanding that the era of armaments has ended and the human race must conform its actions to this truth or die."

"The world no longer has a choice between force and law; if civilization is to survive, it must choose the rule of law."

General Westmaster felt sure he could get the support of other famous American living generals: General Andrew Goodpaster, former Supreme Allied Commander of the European NATO forces and General Lee Butler, the former chief of SAC, the U.S. Strategic Air Command, the air carrier of the atomic weaponry of the U.S.. Both of these generals had publicly gone on record at a Washington Press Conference to demand that the world find a way to eliminate nuclear weapons.

General Westmaster had a plan. He would proceed slowly to perfect it. His task would be to convince the U.S. and the world that the plan could be implemented and would be successful in ending war.

He, like Jim Bucks, had been asked to sit on the Speakers Platform on the night of the celebration in Times Square on New Year's Eve. Unlike Jim, however, he would not have to tell his wife Agnes how to dress. She always dresses appropriately.

COMMANDMENT SEVEN - REVEREND FORGETFUL

"You shall not commit adultery."   Exodus 20:14

"Ken, someone stole my bicycle", Reverend Forgetful spoke to his Head Usher. "I have a suspicion it was one of my parishioners."

"Well", replied Ken, "why don't you preach on the Ten Commandments next Sunday. Maybe the thief will return it out of a guilty conscience."

"That is an excellent idea, Ken", answered the Reverend. "Next Sunday is the last Sunday before the new millennium. What better sermon could there be to start a new millennium, particularly since I have been asked to give the invocation at the Times Square celebration on Friday, New Year's Eve. So on this coming Sunday, upon reading the eighth commandment, 'You shall not steal', I will announce my loss to the congregation, and then pause to give you time to look around at the faces of the congregation to see if anyone looks guilty."

"Sounds like a good plan, Reverend," replied Ken. "I will do my part."

On Sunday, Ken was all prepared to carry out the plan. To his amazement, Reverend Forgetful did not announce his loss to the congregation, nor did he pause at the agreed upon time. Instead, he went right on with his sermon to its conclusion.

After the service, Ken rushed up to the Reverend and demanded an explanation. The Reverend sheepishly responded, "When I read the seventh commandment, 'You shall not commit adultery', I remembered where I had left my bicycle."

COMMANDMENT EIGHT -
SLIGHT OF HAND GANG

"You shall not steal." Exodus 20:15

The Slight of Hand Gang had not been doing too well in their recent pickpocketing trade. Their leader, Antonio Malownofski, drew up plans for his nine-member gang.

Addressing them he said, "Tomorrow night as you know is New Year's Eve, the New Year's Eve that brings in the new millennium. We can make it the New Year's Eve that will bring us the most money ever in one night from our pickpocketing activities. There will be at least 2,000,000 people there. Each of you should be able in one night to pickpocket at least twenty of these people. That means 180 people total. Let's say that we average $50 per person. That will mean $9,000 for the night.

"Let's spread out among the crowd. Art, start in the northwest corner; Will, in the north central part; Max, in the northeast corner; Jock, in the west central part; Craig, in the central center part right in the middle of the whole crowd; Mark, in the east central part; Amos, in the southwestern corner; Mike, in the south central part; and I will take the southeastern corner. Look for the drunks and bump them before relieving them of their wallets. Then let's meet back here after the crowd disperses, but no later than 3:00 a.m. We will divide the spoils then."

COMMANDMENT NINE -
SUZIE TALKLOT

"You shall not bear false witness against your neighbor."
Exodus 20:16

Suzie Talklot: "Mary, I must tell you what I saw happen at the beer bust the other night. Carolyn seduced Kelvin. I couldn't believe my eyes. I saw them leaving the group, so I followed them. They laid down in a secluded spot in a field and made love. She is such a prude. She will never admit to this, but I saw her do it. I couldn't believe it. But don't tell anyone."

Suzie knew Mary could not keep a secret. In fact, Suzie did not want Mary to keep this news secret. Suzie had lied, for all Kelvin and Carolyn had done was to hug and kiss each other while walking along. But Suzie was angry with Carolyn for taking Kelvin's attention away from herself. Within two days Mary had spread the news to six other girls.

Suzie invited Kelvin and Mary, both of whom accepted, to go to Times Square with her on New Year's Eve for the big celebration to bring in the new millennium. She hoped to win back Kelvin's affection and to let Mary see their closeness so Mary could spread the word of this relationship.

COMMANDMENT TEN - BRAD WISHMORE

"You shall not covet your neighbor's house, you shall not covet your neighbor's wife, or male or female slave, or ox, or donkey, or anything that belongs to your neighbor."
Exodus 20:17

Brad Wishmore to his wife Bridget as he was looking out his front window of his home, "Look at our neighbors tonight. All dressed up in a new tux and evening gown. Driving to a party in their brand new Cadillac. I don't know how he does it. I wish I could make money enough to do all they do. The best I can do is to keep us in this house with food and simple clothing. Maybe when I win the lottery we can afford things like theirs.

"Let's go to our no cost party tonight at Times Square. Maybe the new millennium will bring me better luck."

Bridget responded, "Brad, stop coveting others. We have all we need. Money is not everything. It is more important to love our neighbors as ourselves."

Brad replied, "Easy to say, but hard to do when they flaunt their wealth like they do. Anyway, let's get ready for tonight at Times Square on this New Year's Eve."

CHAPTER ELEVEN -
JESUS CHRIST ARRIVES

Two million people cram like sardines into Times Square, New York City, on New Year's Eve, Friday, December 31, 1999 to celebrate the dawn of the Third Millennium. Not a single one there wants to miss this momentous occasion. At the moment, oblivious to the Y2K problem, they want to experience the thrill of this once in a lifetime transfer of time from the Second Millennium to the Third Millennium.

Little do they suspect how momentous it will be.

11:30:00 p.m.

Jim and Denise Bucks, General and Agnes Westmaster, and Reverend Forgetful have taken their respective seats on the platform erected for this occasion. Scattered in the crowd in front of them are Coach Dale McGruff, Larry and Alice Milworth, Walt Brash and his family, Antonio Malownofski and his Slight of Hand Gang, Suzie Talklot with Kelvin and Mary, and Brad and Bridget Wishmore.

11:55:00 p.m.

Reverend Forgetful intones a solemn prayer for the new millennium.

11:58:45 p.m.

"Amen"

11:58:47 p.m.

The eyes of 2,000,000 people focus on the large white
Waterford Crystal Ball at the top of the pole erected for its
descent to reach bottom exactly at midnight.

11:58:48 p.m.

A thunderous clap from a clear sky startles every person there. A heavenly host of angels appear above the crowd singing "Let There be Peace On Earth". A total hush comes over the crowd. The people cannot believe what they are seeing.

11:59:50 p.m.

At the very moment that the white ball should start its descent, a loud explosion scatters the ball into a million pieces of confetti. In its place is Jesus Christ, descending and arriving at the bottom for his triumphal return to Earth, not as described in the Book of Revelation, but as He Himself had decided to make His entrance.

Cheers and prayers rise from the spellbound, now tumultuous crowd. Surrounded by a glow of warmth that makes unnecessary any additional winter clothing, despite the 20-degree outside temperature, Jesus descends quickly, reaching the bottom of the pole at precisely midnight. He walks directly to the microphone and asks to use it. The bewildered Master of Ceremonies with his hand and arm trembling hands the mike to Jesus.

Jesus' voice comes through the mike strong and commanding. "I have returned to Earth as promised to establish My reign of 1,000 years. It is to be a reign of love. 2,000 years ago I lived under the cruel iron fist of the Roman Empire. So first we must establish law and order with freedom and liberty. I have chosen to appear first in New York City for three reasons. First, you are the largest Christian nation in the world; second, the United Nations is headquartered here; and third, the United States is the freest of all nations and the guarantor of freedom and human rights."

"I ask all citizens of the world to elect ten disciples for me within the coming month – two from each color of the races. Color has absolutely nothing to do with the worth of an individual, so we will break down all color and racial biases. Please elect one clergy and one retired government official from each of the five color races – which listed in alphabetical order are black, brown, red, white and yellow. Please elect one male and one female from each color."

"Our goals will be to work with all nations to stop all violence against one another, to eliminate poverty, to abolish war, and to spread love and tolerance throughout the world. God has given you all the knowledge and ability to accomplish these goals in the first 50 years of this millennium, and perhaps even sooner. I have just come from Planet D where we accomplished all this in 49 years.

"God, My Father, has given each of you brains to reason. We will reason together as to the best ways to proceed. After my explanation of how I see us accomplishing the goals I have just enunciated, I will be happy to answer any questions that you might have."

"Over all, you have strayed from the Ten Commandments presented to you from God, My Father, through Moses. My reign will be based on these basic Commandments and the Golden Rule: 'In everything do to others as you would have them do to you ....' Matthew 6:12. The one Commandment that is so frequently ignored is the one I will speak to first. It is the Sixth Commandment that says 'You shall not murder'."

"This last century has seen more people murdered through war and crime and hatred than all other centuries since creation. We must abolish war and turn hatred into love.

"First, we must stabilize the United Nations. As you are aware the UN has no coercive power. It is essentially a forum for all nations to express their views on any and many subjects. Since democracy, with all its faults, is the best form of government yet devised, we should continue to democratize the UN. This means that all dictators must abdicate, their people draw up a democratic constitution, and install a democratic government."

"This will not occur overnight, so we must in the meantime unite all current democracies in a limited federal republic which will include both representative democracy and direct democracy. By direct democracy, I mean the installing of an Initiative/Referendum process in every state and every nation that joins this Union. This is similar to the Initiative/Referendum processes already established in Colorado and California and 22 other states. There are several organizations that are attempting to introduce the Initiative/Referendum process in the other 26 U.S. states and the national government. Two organizations directly involved in educating the American people about this process are the Institute for Initiative/Referendum and Philadelphia II, both based in Washington, DC."

"The main organization educating the populace about a union of democracies is a non-governmental organization by the name of the Association to Unite the Democracies. It is a 59 year old organization started by Clarence Streit, a New York Times reporter during World Wars I & II. In 1939 Streit wrote a book entitled "Union Now" which became a best seller. The book called for the unification of the democracies around the Atlantic to unite politically, militarily, and economically so that they would be so strong that Hitler would never dare to attack. Streit was too late."

"Though the union of democracies has not yet occurred, Streit's organization continues to work toward this goal, with their headquarters in Washington, DC. Over its life of 59 years it has had the support of numerous of your leaders whom you will recognize: President Harry Truman, Senator Estes Kefauver, Under Secretaries of State Will Clayton and Ted Achilles, Secretary of State Christian Herter, Pollster Elmo Roper; Supreme Court Justice Owen Roberts, Presidents Richard Nixon, Dwight Eisenhower, John F. Kennedy; Vice president Hubert Humphrey, Representatives George Bush and Paul Findley, Senator Eugene McCarthy, Speaker of the House James Wright, and many others."

"The European Union could be the core group of democracies to start this process. As soon as they federate, or even before, the other democracies of the North Atlantic Treaty Organization (NATO), the Organization for Economic Cooperation and Development (OECD), and the Organization on Security and Cooperation in Europe (OSCE) should be invited into this Union of Democracies. The United States is the leader in all three of these organizations. After the Union, it is imperative to help Russia democratize and join along with India, South Africa, Mexico, the Central and South American Democracies. All other countries should be invited to join the Union of Democracies as soon as they meet whatever criteria is required by the founding core of the Union."

"By this means within a few years we could have a democratized world, and then disarmament could begin in earnest. The money saved from this reduction in military weaponry could be used to spread love throughout the world through education, hospitals, and human rights observance."

"The Association to Unite the Democracies sponsored a Citizens Constitutional Convention in The Hague, Netherlands in July of 1998. Twenty-seven Participants from 12 European and North American democracies created a good working model for a Constitution for a Union of Democracies which could be used as a starting point for another Constitutional Convention to finalize a draft to be presented to the Peoples of the democracies in referendums."

"Violence of all forms must be stopped. Your US Constitution says it is to protect the lives of its citizens. This overrides the freedom of expression clause and demands that all things possible be done to curb violence, including violent speech, profanity, and violent action.

"You have a national emergency in the US. You kill more people with guns that any other country in the world. Yet you have an organization, the National Rifle Association that is so powerful that it can dictate to congressmen to ignore this. It doesn't matter on which side of the debate you are on, the recommendations for total gun control, greater security checks, stronger enforcement, more policemen - all should be done. Your constitution calls for an armed, well-regulated militia, not the entire citizenry. There should be no militias allowed other than the government regulated national guards.

"I know that General Westmaster is on the platform tonight and I would like for him to come at this time and say a few words. General Westmaster was one of the great leaders in a recent conflict in Europe."

"Jesus, thank you for inviting me to speak. I know that it is believed that your father, God, knows all our thoughts, so certainly he must have known and told you of my thoughts in recent days. Yes, we must abolish war. My thoughts have just been mirrored by what you have said. I will contact this Association to Unite the Democracies immediately and offer my services. When I retire I do intend to give all my spare time to ending war. I have felt that only NATO and its allies would be the ones to do this by politically uniting, but others of the organizations you mentioned could certainly be brought in. We need just one foreign policy from the democracies. And with your support, Jesus, we will not fail to get it. As the non-democracies begin to democratize, the threat of war will diminish until all nations are within the Union of Democracies, at which time all war will end."

"Thank you General Westmaster."

"The next two Commandments I want to address are the First Commandment and at the same time the Second Commandment, because the two are so inter related.

The First Commandment states 'I am the Lord your God.....you shall have no other gods before me.' And the Second supports this, stating, 'You shall not make for yourself an idol, whether in the form of anything that is in heaven above, or that is on the earth beneath, or that is in the water under the earth.....'"

"I submit to you that too many in this world have a Material Idol. They worship the dollar and continue to amass large fortunes after they have more than enough to meet their needs and desires. No person on earth is worth more that one million dollars annually in today's dollars. Poverty should not exist in your country. Yet the gap between the rich and the poor is widening. A more equitable distribution of wealth should be installed to narrow the gap. I trust we will find a way to shrink this gap. All monies earned above the one million dollars per executive per year could be distributed as bonus money among the other employees of the executive's company, or deposited in a fund to help the poor. No person should lack the necessities of food, clothing, shelter, and health care. We could institute programs to insure these benefits are available to all."

" Also we must sap the strength of the multinational cor-
porations which are ruling the world. With their mass of
capital they are able to control the politics of most nations
to the detriment of the poor."

"We should find a way to gainfully employ every person in the world. To help with this there must be birth control, for your planet can support only so many people, something less that what we have today. Your God gave you the ability to procreate, but he also gave you the means to control this. No unwanted child should be brought into this world. I plan to speak with the Pope about this matter."

"There is another pervasive idol that has emerged in the world since WWII. That is the Sex Culture idol. I will say more about this when I speak on the Seventh Commandment.

" Mr. Jim Bucks, President and CEO of Corporation X, a Fortune 500 Company, is with us on this platform. I ask him to come say a few words at this time".

"Jesus, I am almost speechless. I have never looked at my life in the manner you described. But my idol is material wealth. I confess it. It is the measure of success in our country. But I will change my way of living, for what you say is true. I will continue working for Corporation X as long as it will have me, and I will forget retirement and its attendant Golden Parachute. My wife and I will reduce our assets to one million dollars and give the remainder (over $100,000,000 now) to charities helping the poor.

"Particularly I want to help the charities that are helping the poor to learn the wherewithal to support themselves. I believe in the phrase "Give a man a fish and he will be fed for one day, but teach a man to fish and he will have food as long as he lives.

"I will also cut my salary to $1,000,000 per year and divide the remaining salary I have been getting in an annual bonus to our employees. Thank you Jesus for opening my eyes. I will support you 100% in your reign.

"Thank you Mr. Bucks."

"The Seventh Commandment, 'You shall not commit adultery' is the next topic I will address."

"I mentioned that I would talk about the Sex Culture when I talked about adultery. Adultery is pre-marital sex or out of wedlock sex. The acceptance of the Sex Culture since WWII is due to the media - magazines, books, Internet, movies, TV, advertisers - blatantly destroying the Puritan moral code of pre-WWII through nudity, profanity, and innuendo. These have also caused the horrible increase in rape and sexual assault, often ending in physical harm or murder. The parents of today need to instill the values of their own grandparents into their progeny if we are to stop the evils of the Sex Culture."

" The specter of homosexuality has emerged in the public eye. God never intended for such sexuality. His purpose in having male and female was to ensure the continuation of the human race. If two men or two women believe that they must forego the pleasure of a normal marriage of male and female, then it should be by the same commitment rules as in the normal marriage, i.e. there should be only one partner for each until death does part. There should also be no pre relationship sexual activity. Homosexuals should not flaunt their kind of relationship and should not expect or demand any additional privileges over what others have."

"Reverend Forgetful is on the platform with us tonight. I ask him to please come forward and say a few words. While he is talking I invite coach Dale McGruff, Mr. Larry Milworth, Teenager Walt Brash, Gang Leader Antonio Malownofski, Ms. Suzie Talklot, and Brad Wishmore to please work their way to the platform. I know that they are out there in the crowd.

"Jesus, before you and God and all these people before us and those watching us on TV, I confess my sin of adultery. I am ashamed of it, I do repent, and I beg yours and God's forgiveness. I promise this will never again happen to me. And I want to say to all my fellow clergymen wherever you may be, do not commit adultery. You are the role models for your parishioners and your denominational members. Do not let them down by disobeying God's Commandment."

"Thank you, Reverend Forgetful. You are forgiven."

"The next commandment I want to address is the Third Commandment - 'You shall not make wrongful use of the name of the Lord your God.'

"Cursing is a useless waste of words and time. Before WWII there was a censorship board in the US called the Hayes Committee. No cursing was allowed in movies. The Committee gave special permission to Rhett Butler in the movie "Gone With the Wind " to end the movie with its only curse word, "Frankly, my Dear, I don't give a damn." Freedom of speech should also require Responsibility. The profanity in movies, songs, books, and magazines is far too excessive. Its use should be curtailed through a Responsibility Amendment to the Constitution.

"I see that Coach Dale McGruff has come to the platform to say a few words. He is the coach and the role model for his football team."

"Jesus, as did Reverend Forgetful, I too want to ask for yours and God's forgiveness for my taking his name in vain so many times in my life, and particularly on the football field where I am trying to indoctrinate my players with the ethics of the game. Certainly their speech is part of this. Henceforth I will pledge to curtail all my damn curse words; (whoops! I mean all my curse words), and replace them with appropriate English language. It will be difficult for me to do , but I will do it. I urge everyone hearing me tonight to follow Jesus' advice and clean up his or her act."

"Thank you Coach McGruff. You are forgiven."

"Number Four is the next Commandment I will address. 'Remember the Sabbath day, and keep it holy. Six days you shall labor, and do all your work. But the seventh day is a Sabbath to the Lord your God: you shall not do any work'....."

"When is your Sabbath? It does not matter which day you set aside to rest and contemplate. If you attend church regularly, then the day your church calls its Sabbath could be yours. If you do not attend church regularly, then pick out a day of the week that fits into your work schedule. Use this day for resting, recreation, contemplating, family enjoyment, and spiritual enhancement. Resist being a workaholic. I have asked Mr. Larry Milworth to come to the platform and say a few words."

"Jesus, thank you for opening my eyes to my being a workaholic. I had not thought of it in that way before. Yes I enjoy working, but I have neglected my family because of my work leaving no time for them. As of today I will set aside at least one day each week to be with my family, to rest, and to seek spiritual enhancement."

"Thank you Mr. Milworth."

" 'Honor your father and your mother, so that your days may be long on the land that the Lord your God is giving you' is the Fifth and next Commandment that I will address."

"Parents, you are the front line in the rearing of your children. It does take a community to raise and guide the children, but you have the awesome responsibility on the front line. Children, as long as your parents are paying your way you must honor and obey them except in those few instances where you know they are leading you into immoral or criminal activity. I think all responsible parents would like to see their children stay drug free, alcohol free, abstain from smoking, and abstain from sexual activity until married. Also, following the Boy Scout Code of being trustworthy, loyal, helpful, friendly, courteous, kind, obedient, cheerful, thrifty, brave, clean and reverent will please every parent. Listen and obey.

"Being one of the thousands of teenagers in the crowd, Walt Brash has come to the platform to say a few words."

"Jesus, I disobeyed my father by taking his car without his permission to a Kegger where I drank beer heavily, wrecked the car on the way home, and seriously hurt one of my friends. Here in public and before you and God I confess my sin and promise to work with Dad and Mother and to follow their directions and rules to the best of my ability. I do understand that they have had more experience than I. I will also stop my beer drinking. I will also refrain from using drugs and from smoking, and will remain a virgin until married."

"Thank you Walt, You are forgiven."

"The Eighth Commandment is 'You shall not steal'."

"Stealing is a crime that afflicts every nation. We will hear from the leader of a gang of pickpockets tonight, for I see Antonio Malownofski has come to our platform. But before we hear from him I want to say that Pickpocketing is just one form of stealing. There are so many other kinds, that we cannot explore them all tonight. But let us list a few. Shoplifting, car theft, jewelry theft, art theft, bank and business holdups, income tax cheating, home robbery, securities fraud, etc.,etc. Here again you parents are in the front line to teach your children to never steal in any form. Respect for other people's properties is a fundamental block upon which our Society is grounded. In the coming Millennium we must do all in our power to put an end to all forms of theft. And now it is time for Antonio to speak to you."

"Jesus, because of our fear of You and Your power and because of admiration for You in Your quest to bring Heaven to Earth, I want to announce that I want every member of my Slight of Hand Gang to cease all pick-pocketing immediately, to return all that you may have already seized. If you cannot find your victim, bring your loot to the platform here and meet with any victim that has not had his wallet or money returned to him within the next hour. I know that we are guilty of a crime here, but I beg your forgiveness and plead with the police here to help us return the stolen valuables without arresting us, but letting us go free to change the name of our gang to Gang for Christ. We will do whatever Jesus wants us to do to help wipe out crime. We henceforth will be Crimestoppers."

"Thank you Antonio. I do forgive you. I want to meet with you and your gang tomorrow to map out a program for you to implement your crimestopping. I will ask the Chief of Police to join us to give us his input and blessing."

"The next to the last Commandment, the Ninth, states 'You shall not bear false witness against your neighbor'."

"How often through gossip do stories of others become embellished into untruths or half-truths. At all times we must strive to tell the whole truth, nothing but the truth, so help us God. We have a young lady who violated this Commandment this week. I ask Ms. Suzie Talklot to please come forward to say a few words."

"Jesus, I am embarrassed to stand before this huge audience and particularly before my boyfriend, Kelvin, who is here to hear what I am about to say. I apologize to you Kelvin because I told a lie about you and Carolyn to our friend Mary. I wanted to disgrace Carolyn so that you would pay more attention to me. It was wrong for me to do this and I beg for forgiveness from you, Carolyn, Jesus and God. Please forgive me."

Tears rolled down the cheeks of Suzie as she returned to her seat next to Kelvin, who squeezed her hand. Carolyn, who was not at Times Square would have to be told on the morrow.

"You are forgiven Suzie. Thank you for your confession. Go forth and bear no more false witness against anyone."

"The final Commandment number Ten deals with relationships with your neighbors. It states 'You shall not covet your neighbor's house; you shall not covet your neighbor's wife, or male or female slave, or ox, or donkey, or anything that belongs to your neighbor'."

"Coveting is the next worse thing to stealing. You are wishing for something that belongs to someone else, but you are at least good enough not to steal.

"There are parts of the Bible that do need to be updated. Its tolerance of slavery is no longer true. You have fought a war within this country to end the ownership of slaves. However in some parts of the world, slavery is still allowed, or tolerated if not legal. Every human is entitled to life, liberty, and the pursuit of happiness. Slavery of all types must be abolished. I have asked Brad Wishmore to say a few words."

"Jesus, I certainly do not covet anyone's slave, but I do confess that I have coveted the material wealth of my neighbor and I do believe that we must close the gap between the rich and the poor. I think that if we do close that gap there will be considerably less coveting. I do ask for your forgiveness and tomorrow I will apologize to my neighbor. Henceforth I will make sure that I enjoy the blessings that I do have and quit coveting."

"Thank you, Mr. Wishmore. You are forgiven."

"So there you have the Ten Commandments of God. There is one other I will add and that is the Golden Rule, which I stated in my Sermon on the Mount, 'In everything do to others as you would have them do to you.' This rule alone if practiced by everyone would end wars. But until everyone abides by this rule, we must bring about law and order under the political system. The best for this is the Union of Democracies as I have expressed before."

"Yes, God my Father, and I appreciate your respect for Us and your worship of Us, but we expect far more in your deeds of love and compassion. We do not have to have all the adoration you bestow upon Us. Place more of this on your family and friends.

"So we have now entered the Third Millennium. It will be the Millennium in which we bring Heaven to Earth. We will conquer Satan and banish him from this Planet. Welcome to Paradise to come.

"Now that I have explained in general terms how my reign will bring about peace, love and compassion, the abolition of violence, and the abolition of poverty, I will answer any questions that you might have."

CHAPTER 12 - QUESTIONS & ANSWERS

Question #1

"From whence did you come?"

"I came from Planet D where we have established a heaven on it.

"I was transported here at the speed of light, which is 186,000 miles per second, and I will remain here for 1,000 years as ordered by My Father."

Question #2

"Where will you have your office?"

"I will move from country to country to work with my disciples and to talk with religious leaders, governmental leaders, and civil society. I had no office when I lived on Earth 2,000 years ago. I will work closely with my ten disciples who will have separate areas of administration. But as you have witnessed, I have the ability to move quickly from place to place."

Question #3

"How will you get other religions to cooperate with you?"

"Over time I believe we can show that Christianity is compatible with all other religions. My coming will help to solidify the religions. By convincing the peoples of the various lands that democracy is the best form of civil government, it would follow that our religion of love and peace will complement other religions to the extent that we can work harmoniously with them."

Question #4

"Do you still believe that abiding by the Ten Commandments is the best guide for human actions?"

"Yes. The Ten Commandments and My Sermon on the Mount, which includes the Golden Rule: 'In everything do to others as you would have them do to you' , are the best guide for successful living."

Question #5

"What is your definition of successful living?"

"A man or a woman is very successful if he or she grows up drug free, (including cigarettes and alcohol) crime free, abides by the Ten Commandments and the Golden Rule, marries into a happy, loving relationship that lasts till death does part, raises children lovingly, and provides the bare necessities of food, shelter, and clothing. The amount of money he, she, or they earn does not matter as long as it is sufficient for the bare necessities of life."

Question #6

"Who will be your disciples?"

"You will elect one black clergy and one black retired government official, one brown clergy and one brown retired government leader, and likewise with the other three racial colors - red, white, and yellow. Five will be men and five will be women."

Question #7

"What is your position on abortion?"

"Abortion is a last resort. First, there should be no inter-course prior to marriage. Second, there should be no adultery after marriage. Third, no unwanted child should be brought into the world. Fourth, life begins when the umbilical cord is severed. For the safety of the earth's environment and the health of its citizens, population control must be exercised through abstinence prior to marriage and birth control means after marriage."

Question # 8

"Will the democratic Union of the Democracies be like the United States or like the European Union or like the Swiss Confederation?"

"The Union I suggest will be a federal union most similar to the United States. One new feature could be Direct Democracy through voting on Initiatives by the People and on Referendums from the Legislature. Your modern technology makes people voting once a month on important issues feasible and practical."

"Let us now lift up a prayer for the coming millennium. I know none better than the one I taught My disciples 2,000 years ago. Please note in the prayer that we will bring Heaven to Earth. I will see to it during my 1,000 year reign. Please bow your heads and join with me in this prayer:

"Our Father, who art in Heaven, hallowed be thy name. Thy kingdom come, thy will be done, on Earth as it is in Heaven. Give us this day our daily bread, and forgive us our trespasses as we forgive those who trespass against us. Lead us not into temptation, but deliver us from evil, for thine is the kingdom, and the power, and the glory forever. Amen."

In the split second it took for the 2,000,000 people to look up from their bowed heads, Jesus was gone.